MW00889336

Copyright ©2019 by Keely Edwards. Keely Edwards retains sole copyright to all text and visual material in this publication. Any reprint or duplication is prohibited without the express permission of the author.

www.keelyedwards.website • keelyedwards@yahoo.com

Why do you just sit and stare
in the shadows by the
archway Cobalt?

Why do you peer out over the valley with only a silent glare?

We miss your gentle words and your thoughts of care.

No more chats by the statues
and talks by the fountain.

No more laughing by the post office
or sharing our day as we walk down
the mountain.

Tamari,
you do not know
what has occurred?

*When I said that Etta's
feathers were full . . .*

*she said that I called her fat, plump, and
obese in a mouthful.*

When I told Roscoe the Cat
that his eyes were
so deep brown . . .

He said that I said they were ugly and then he repeated it to all, one-by-one, all around.

Cobalt I know you, your heart is true.

You would reach out and touch all creatures with your words of love anew.

Share once again by the
fountain, valleys
and archways.

Tell me about all of the wonders on your adventures and pathways.

Brighten our days
with your
words of beauty.

With shining eyes,
Cobalt softly promises, "I will, I will."

I dedicate my children's book to Cousin Vincent and Jo, Cousin Karolyn and Gervis, Cousin Carolyn, Christina, and my nephew Vincent. Each one sharing their life and love with their children, grandchildren, great-grandchidren and/or great-great-grandchildren.

I also dedicate Cobalt's story to Glen and Sheri who allowed me to visually capture their rescue dog Tamari so that she could become Cobalt's best friend. More adventures are ahead for Tamari and Cobalt.

42191582R00018

Made in the USA
Middletown, DE
12 April 2019

ISBN 9781798687932